The

Beryl Bumblebee

Beryl Flies High

THE ADVENTURES OF BERYL BUMBLEBEE

BERYL FLIES HIGH

Written and illustrated by
S Amos

The Adventures of Beryl Bumblebee: Beryl Flies High
S. Amos

Published by Aspect Design 2013
Malvern, Worcestershire, United Kingdom.

Designed and Printed by Aspect Design
89 Newtown Road, Malvern, Worcs. WR14 1PD
United Kingdom
Tel: 01684 561567
E-mail: allan@aspect-design.net
Website: www.aspect-design.net

A copy of this book has been deposited with the British Library Board

ISBN 978-1-908832-35-1

Beryl Flies High

Beryl was the most beautiful bumblebee ever. She had a soft furry body, striped with black and bright yellow and knew just how beautiful she looked. She was always admiring herself in the mirror.

7

Beryl Bumblebee was a worker bee. That meant she flew out of the nest each day to find pollen and nectar to bring back home. All her sisters did the same and there were lots of them!

Their home was a small nest under the floorboards of our garden shed. The Queen Bee always decided where they would build their nest and this year, it happened to be under our garden shed!

One morning in June when the sun was rising giving hope to a really hot day, Beryl and her sisters trundled around the garden collecting pollen and nectar in their pollen baskets which are on their hind legs.

When they had collected enough they took it to the Queen Bee who used it first of all to line the nest. Once the nest was completed she then used it for feeding her children.

Beryl then returned to our garden and was buzzing around happily settling on the sweet peas Grandpa had planted earlier.

She had already learned how to get nectar out of the flowers. It was easy to do in some flowers, like the daisy, but we didn't have many daisies in our garden because Daddy liked to keep the grass cut short.

Beryl, like all other bumblebees, had to learn how to get inside the various flowers because they all had different shapes. She preferred to visit certain species of flowers lots of times. This is what they called 'Consistency.'

As she moved from pink sweet peas to purple ones, she spied a frog sitting on a stone underneath the flowers.

'Oh, Oh!' she thought to herself.

She knew that this could mean trouble because frogs loved to eat bumblebees. You would think that they would be afraid of being stung, but they looked forward to a delicious meal when they caught sight of a bumblebee within their reach.

Beryl kept her sting in her tail. Only the girl bumblebees had stings, and, of course, the Queen Bee also had a sting, but the boys didn't.

The frog watched Beryl for quite a long time and Beryl watched the frog too!

Suddenly the frog jumped off the stone alarming Beryl causing her to instinctively fly upwards.

She found herself flying higher and higher until the sweet peas became little dots and the roof of the shed became so small she could hardly see it.

She seemed to be carried up and up and no amount of flapping her four wings could make her change direction.

Up, up she was lifted and sailed across the countryside. There were only a few clouds that day so she was able to look down on tiny houses, roads that looked like ribbons and trees that looked like little green blobs.

She was lifted higher and higher until she couldn't see much at all. She was getting caught up in small cotton wool clouds, which were soft and refreshing as they touched her face.

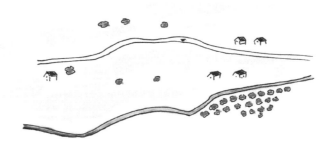

Beryl began to get worried. Would she ever be able to get back to earth? Where would she end up? Would her mother miss her? Would her brothers and sisters try to find her?

Then, the clouds opened to reveal the most beautiful garden. The fragrance of flowers filled Beryl's scent detectors in her antennae. She could drink such delicious nectar and eat as much pollen as she could manage. Oh how wonderful!

She fluttered on to the largest iris she had ever seen. The petals opened up like an umbrella and there she rested on a pink petal, drinking until she couldn't move.

She lay on the huge petal and gazed above at a sky that looked like a large precious stone. Everywhere glittered and shone. This must be heaven! The colours were brilliant, that is, all except the red flowers. Bumblebees cannot see the colour red.

But, how could she get back to the nest that the Queen Bee had lovingly made, that she had moulded and sealed with wax so that she could lay her eggs? How could Beryl get back to see the baby bumblebees hatch and eat their way out of that nest?

She began to cry. This beautiful garden was truly wonderful, but she did so long to be back with her family.

She would tell them all about this adventure if only she knew how to get back down to earth again.

She didn't see another bee anywhere and there were

no other insects. She was alone in this enormous, beautiful place. There was no-one to ask.

What could she do?

She had been given an opportunity to see the most magnificent garden in the world but would gladly exchange that for the humble nest under our garden shed.

Beryl had never travelled so far and to be up in the heavens was so out of character for any bee. She was used to hibernating under the ground in winter so this was a completely new experience.

Suddenly her antennae felt a huge vibration and before she knew it, everywhere was lit up. It was like a big fireworks display with sparkles and flashes everywhere.

Then the clouds underneath her opened up and fine water fell upon her fluffy coat.

She felt herself gliding. First of all, she moved gently away from the garden, then began to fall very, very slowly.

Quite soon she was able to see tiny blobs on the earth's surface which became bigger and bigger.

She was coming home! Yes! She really was coming home!

Was all this a dream?

She landed on our lawn and buzzed quickly into the nest, no doubt to tell all her mother and brothers and sisters all about her adventure.

Do you think they will believe it?